PREPARING FOR PRESSURE

Frank Giampaolo

CONTENTS

FOREWORD

Frank's new book is powerful! It's an eye-opener that will reshape your approach to the game. In *Preparing for Pressure*, he explains why some players thrive under pressure, while others break down, and provides readers with remedial tools.

Coaches, parents, and athletes will be enlightened as Frank leads his readers on a journey to understand why preparing for pressure is a mandatory component of the competitive game. Focusing only on a player's strokes and athleticism, disregarding preparation for the mental and emotional aspects of the sport, is a common coaching oversight. *Preparing for Pressure* gives you the tools to fill that gap.

Frank's knowledge is matched only by his passion for sharing his insights with his fellow coaches to help players reach their full potential. In *Preparing for Pressure*, Frank has written what I'm certain will be another bestseller.

Julie Jilly
VP Marketing & Events
PTR

PREFACE

Preparing for Pressure came to light organically. It began as a Professional Tennis Registry (PTR) Tennis Pro Magazine instructional article and quickly ballooned into a full-blown book.

Those of you familiar with my earlier works will notice a consistent theme, which is to be a solution-oriented educator. Identifying a problem is elementary. Providing the appropriate solution customized to the athlete is genius. *Preparing for Pressure* was written to provide solutions to assist those athletes who are able to thrive on the practice court only to wilt under game-day pressure. I've found that performing well under pressure begins with preparing the athlete's software (mental and emotional components) for the heaviness of competition.

Athletes who have ignored software development exhibit pre-match anxieties such as agitation, frustration, excuse oriented dialog, stomach sickness and psychosomatic injuries, self-doubt, jealousy, and envy.

"Many athletes have the will to groove their fundamental skills, but they often fail to prepare properly for pressure."

Preparing for Pressure was written to counter the assumption that winning is everything. Children witness the attention and accolades received by winners, and they want it. To the naive, winning equates to personal self-worth. It's hammered into each of us via TV, social media, school, and through youth sports. Of course, everyone wants to be a winner, but not everyone is willing to prepare for the ugliness of competition.

The US Navy SEAL's motto, **"We don't rise to the occasion…we sink to the level of our training,"** best describes performing under pressure.

The often debilitating scenario athlete's face during competition is remedied with deliberate mental and emotional training. Athletes aren't born competitive tennis experts. Performing their best when they need it the most is nurtured.

With observational candor, humor, and decades of experience, I shed light on exactly why most competitors are spectators after the early rounds. And provide solutions to performing at their peak performance under pressure.

INTRODUCTION

Preparing athletes for pressure is a form of preventative medicine. It inoculates athletes with solutions for common performance anxieties. The solutions vaccinate the athlete, coaches, and parents against the onslaught of emotional toxins found in competition.

"Every athlete feels pressure; it is how they've been nurtured to deal with it that counts."

Preparing for Pressure is a guide to assist coaches, parents, and players through the process of inventorying their athlete's software faculties. It offers deep insights into the often ignored mental and emotional components. This book begins with the Clarity of Pressure, through the Coaches Pathway, into the Parental Vision and concludes with Common Performance Anxieties.

NOTE: The following book content may be considered "Information Overload" to the intermediate parent or coach. It is my intent to provide the reader with too much, rather than not enough information.

Mastery of performing under pressure on the tennis court begins with the insights found within the following pages. While reading through the insights, I encourage you to recognize your athlete's level of competence and confidence within each skill set, which will determine the best path for maximum improvement.

Learning is most productive when the instructor is able to communicate to the athlete's level. Expert educators get into their student's world instead of demanding that their students get into their world.

The basis to all learning stems from recognizing the following four stages of enlightenment:

1) **Unconscious Incompetence**—Doing something wrong and not knowing it is wrong.

2) **Conscious Incompetence**—Doing something wrong but knowing it is wrong.

3) **Conscious Competence**—Doing something right but forced to focus on doing it right.

4) **Unconscious Competence**—Doing something right and repeating it without effort or thought.

Whether it is realized or not, all successful learning passes through these four stages of enlightenment. The goal is to perform in stage four-**Unconscious Competence.**

Preparing for Pressure teaches life skills, positive character traits, and morals covertly. Ultimately, nurtured positive life skills maximize potential. This book dives into the fields of sports science and psychology. Frank offers 30 years of bold, inspired solutions and connective storytelling as he organized the content for easy reading. Enjoy.

CLARITY OF PRESSURE

I've been intrigued for decades with the reoccurring topic, "Why certain athletes thrive under pressure, while others wilt." Researching high achievers, such as Navy SEAL's, professional athletes, Olympians, and CEO's of major corporations, I found high achievers perform at their peak level when it matters most because they routinely prepare very different than the intermediate athlete.

Clarity of Pressure was written to highlight the fact that pressure affects performance. All too often, parents and coaches sidestep the actual training of software in favor of grooving ground-strokes. This common training scenario leaves the athlete unknowingly unprepared for pressure.

The athlete's sphere of influence would be wise to actively shape the athlete's future. The software needed to thrive under stress doesn't develop by chance. Mental and emotional skill sets need to be developed and nurtured routinely. The confidence we seek comes from developing character, not just mechanics. Consistently promoting strong work ethic, effort, tenacity, optimism, and organization are the character traits found in champions.

WHAT IS COMPETITIVE TENNIS PRESSURE?

"Competitive pressure is the lousy partner of great opportunity."

In amateur sports, pressure is either self-imposed or nurtured by unaware parents or coaches. Pressure manifests when we imagine what might happen if we don't achieve the outcome we desire or what others expect.

Like clockwork, Brian's frustration begins before each tournament match. This solid athlete can't understand why he's not able to duplicate his practice level in tournament competition. Friday on the practice court, Brian grooves his fundamental groundstrokes for hours. Essentially playing "catch" back and forth. In this setting, Brian thinks, "Tennis is easy. Forget juniors...Man, I'm going pro!"

Fast forward to Saturday morning. Brian's internal and external stressors ramp up because the practice court environment of catch is nowhere to be found. The friendly face on the other side of the net is now replaced by an intimidating, confrontational warrior who is determined to torture poor Brian. Come game day, that cozy, cooperative game of "catch" turns into a violent struggle of "keep away." Brian would be wise to practice in the manner he's expected to perform. This requires practicing "keep away," delivering and receiving on the move. In addition to stationary fundamental stroke development.

Preparing for Pressure # 1 Rule: Practice in the manner you're expected to perform.

WHAT CAUSES PRESSURE IN COMPETITION?

"Performance anxiety is the habit of worrying."

Pressure begins with the arrival of the athlete's inner critic. That little "Devil on their shoulder" appears like clockwork when the match doesn't go as planned. Some athletes stress about every minute detail while others confront setbacks in warrior mode. Due to the fact that no two athletes are exactly alike, preparing for pressure begins with an assessment of the athlete's and their entourage's stress level as it pertains to the reality of tournament competition.

Competitive Pressure Triggers Include:

1. The Games Scoring System

2. The Opponents Style of Tactical Play

3. Gamesmanship

4. The Draw/Seeding

5. Spectators

6. The Environment/Conditions

7. The Court Surface

8. Current Fitness/Energy Levels

9. Untrustworthy Strokes

10. Outcome Anxieties

I've found that taking an inventory and talking through possible tennis stressors, in a mental/emotional training session, is a great start to overcoming issues and developing confident solutions. Which of the preceding ten triggers cause pressure for your athletes?

Identifying the athlete's personal stressors leads to a customized developmental plan which will maximize their potential.

WHAT IS CONFIDENCE?

"Confidence isn't about thinking you're better than everyone else...it's about believing that you've prepared yourself to be the very best you can be."

At every event, we see a version of cocky Craig. Craig arrives on site with his Nike hat on backward, his "ginormous" 8-pack HEAD bag on his shoulders. He struts through the clubhouse as he spins a racket on his right index finger. Cocky Craig goes down in flames first round most tournaments due to his lack of proper preparation.

Confidence allows athletes to trust their thoughts and abilities. Athletes who are sure about their style of play, most proficient patterns, and clarity of situational solutions have prepared themselves for pressure.

Are your athletes well versed in their most proficient styles of play, patterns, and on-court strategic solutions? Typically, unconfident athletes focus on the possible catastrophe ahead, while confident athletes look forward to the challenge.

Confidence is built on proper preparation. It's the feeling of knowing you have the solutions when things go astray.

PARENTAL CONFIDENCE

"High rankings are achieved and sustained through consistent weekly growth."

Mrs. Chen and her son William walk into their tennis session with one thing on their mind – William's rankings. "How do we get to #3, SCTA?" "Which UTR should we play to maximize his points?" 'Do we get more points from an L -2 in Southern California or a D-2 in El Paso Texas?' While understanding the current ranking process is important, the ranking based approach to improvement can stunt the growth of an athlete. It's like putting the cart before the horse. Unfortunately, it's not the cart that's propelling the journey, it's the horse. In the Chen family's world, the cart is the rankings, and the horse is his customized developmental plan.

Outcome and ranking obsession adds unnecessary stress that takes a toll on the athlete's physical, mental, and emotional preparation and performances. In reality, focusing on the results is a distraction to the improvement process. Once parents and athletes shift their attention to building skills, they'll develop the tools needed to get the results they seek. And the athlete and the entourage will begin to enjoy the journey instead of hoping for future happiness. Real confidence is gained on the path of mastery. Under pressure, confidence is the #1 reported skill parents and athletes seek.

When parents and athletes focus their attention and energy less on the results and more on the processes, they maximize potential at a quicker rate.

OVER-CONFIDENCE VS UNDER-CONFIDENCE

"Under-confidence in match play is often a result of false-confidence in preparation."

Let's look deeper into a pre-tournament conversation with our friend Cocky Craig:

Frank: *"Craig, Did you review your audio tapes/mental rehearsals?"*
Craig: *"Nah..., I'm good."*
Frank: *"Craig, Did you play your practice matches this week?"*
Craig: *"I forgot to call-em in time, and they already had plans."*
Frank: *"Craig, Did you do your off-court cardio routine?"*
Craig: *"No, I'm sore from last Mondays hit. I didn't want to get injured."*

Signs of Over-Confidence in Athletes:

- Avoids Pre-Match Preparation
- Avoids Off-Court Training
- Lacks Secondary Strokes
- Avoids Playing Sets
- Unrealistic Outcome Goals

Signs of Appropriate Confidence in Athletes:

- Grit
- Relaxed Breathing
- Millisecond Problem Solving Skills
- Perseverance
- Resiliency
- Determination
- Smiling

Signs of Under-Confidence in Athletes:

- Choking/Panicking
- Shallow/Heavy Breathing
- Impaired Memory
- Anger/Indifference
- Tight Muscle Contractions
- Impulsive-Irrational Decision Making
- Pessimism

Confidence fortifies... but overconfidence and under-confidence destroys.

CONFIDENCE BIAS: THE FALSE REALITY

"Pre-match over confidence leads to match day under confidence."

Athletes and parents often have skewed opinions of their competitive skill levels. Is it because Molly, once held her own against a much higher level opponent in a practice set in 2019? Or maybe because Mrs. Johnson watches her son Zack hit beautiful groundstrokes while his coach feeds balls right into his strike zone for the entire lesson. These false leaders cause skewed opinions from parents and athletes.

Confidence bias leads to an inaccurate belief in one's true competitive skill sets. The concern with over-confidence is that the athlete is positive that they have all the skills necessary to compete supremely without actually ever training those skills. False reality result in devastating losses and blame games. The opposite, under-confidence, bias also wreaks havoc under pressure. Some well-trained athletes suffer from their lack of confidence in competition; harboring unjustified negative beliefs or nurtured undermining pessimistic viewpoints. Either way, their lack of self-esteem seriously affects their performance.

The good news is that with proper software development, false confidence from both the parents and the athlete can be re-wired. Re-routing inner dialog through self-coaching is a great start. Athletes who suffer from confidence bias would be wise to trade in some of their hours grooving groundstrokes and replace them with solution-based software sessions.

Preparing for pressure includes the awareness of the athlete's confidence bias. Allowing false belief systems leads to future anguish.

Come tournament day false confidence sabotages.

TRAIN OPTIMISTIC SELF-DIALOG

"Outer-change begins with inner-change."

Our minds create an ongoing inner dialog. Sadly, once competition begins, far too many athlete's inner-conversation is negative and downright abusive. Do you know any competitors whose internal communications routinely convince them that they're unworthy?

Self-coaching requires awareness of our thoughts, words, and actions. With awareness, athletes can override their pessimistic chatter and turn it into solution-based optimism. Athletes with positive inner dialog radiate confidence, and real confidence is what is needed under pressure.

On a daily basis, I encourage parents and athletes to "Flip it" whenever they pick up negative facial expressions, body language, or pessimistic chatter. During my sessions, I allow each participant in group settings to smile and say "Flip it!" to any other athlete whose displaying "poor me" behaviors. It's amazing that by simple awareness, these negatrons decrease their unwanted demeanor. Try the "Flip it" game and change pessimists into optimists.

ATHLETIC HISTORY IS TRANSFERABLE

"All athletes don't start from the same starting line."

A few years back, I taught a semi-private beginners clinic for two women that had never played tennis, Margarete and Kaylin. Margarete was a 20-year accountant. She had never participated in any sport. Standing to her left was Kaylin. She was a 3-Time Olympian Gold Medalist in Swimming. Kaylin spent countless hours each week developing her physical, mental, and emotional competitive skills.

These two beginners had very different athletic histories. Do you think applying the same developmental plan for these two beginners would be appropriate? Not a chance, they are worlds apart in their athletic experience.

It pays to evaluate each individual's athletic history before simply feeding balls to your students. Preparing athletes for competition requires customization based on their individual athletic experience. While technical skills are usually unique to the sport, mechanical transfers occasionally transfer. An example is when a baseball/softball player has trained the biomechanics of their throwing motion, which shares several technical skills of a service motion. The essential mental and emotional skills of a high-performance competitor are often interchangeable, such as life skills and the positive character traits needed at the elite levels of any sport.

Examples include time management, courage, resiliency, work ethic, and perseverance. Understanding this transfer principle saves valuable training time while accelerating results.

Athletes enter the sport with varying degrees of athletic history.

IS YOUR ATHLETE A WORRIER OR WARRIOR?

Customize Training Based on Mindset

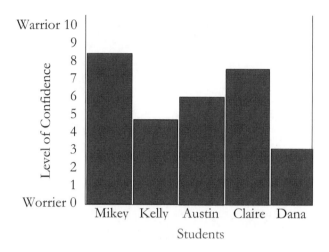

The above emotional developmental chart documents the level of anxieties each athlete carries into competition. Emotional development significantly affects how each individual handles stress and prepares for pressure. Some are born warriors, some are born worriers, but most fall somewhere in between. Though each individual is born with a genetic predisposition toward competitiveness, one's nature is not the sole influence. The way in which they were nurtured also molds their behaviors.

The nurturing style of an athlete's parents plays a crucial role in their competitiveness. Athletes enter into the sport with predispositions and life skill experiences. This is why customized training is paramount.

Excessive worrying compromises one's physical, mental, and emotional abilities.

MASTERY REQUIRES LEAVING ONE'S COMFORT ZONE

"Pushing through the walls of fear is the path towards mastery."

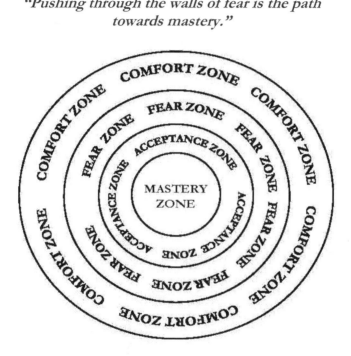

Mastering requires the athlete to accept that leaving their comfort zone is often uncomfortable because it forces the athlete to punch through their walls of disbelief and doubt. Mastering one's own emotions comes before mastering the competitive game. The mental barrier of not believing in themselves is what keeps most athletes from attempting new skills and ultimately competing well under stress.

It's within the job description of the athlete's sphere of influence to help navigate the athlete through their walls of self-doubt, fear, and disbelief.

Progress is found on the other side of each athlete's invisible walls that are holding them hostage. Gaining mastery of the physical, mental, and emotional skills requires consistent targeted training and the enjoyment of the process. Mastery takes place only after thousands of hours of deliberate practice.

Mastery isn't a function of sheer athleticism. It's a function of courage, deliberate focus, perseverance, and work ethics.

COGNITIVE CONTROL

"Great competitors don't just control the ball...they control their wandering minds."

Preparing for pressure requires the ability to avoid meltdowns. The athletes wandering mind is a precursor to the bad patches that are often present in match play. Just because the athlete is physically standing on court #6 in tournament competition, doesn't mean his/her mind is present. In intermediate tennis, thoughts routinely drift from past to present to future sabotaging their performance.

RANDOM FOCUS CHART		
PAST	PRESENT	FUTURE
Mistake	Global Strategy	Next Opponent
Confrontations	Tactics	Ranking
Ranking	Opponent	Trophy
Seeding	Profiling	Parents Views
Successes	Rituals	Friends Views
Failures	Routines	Lunch
	Optimism	Homework

Match-time meltdowns typically start when an athlete fails to stay in the moment. Staying in the present, focusing on performance goals is a crucial asset for the mentally strong athlete. It's important to note that even the top athletes lose focus. The difference is that the seasoned competitors recognize the mental drift and quickly return to their script.

Lucky for most junior players, losing focus for a moment won't make them lose the match. What does cause serious trouble is being unable to refocus and get back on script. It's safe to say that preparing for pressure includes eliminating mental interferences.

Performing well under pressure requires that the athlete recognize when their mind travels away from the task at hand.

BLAME SHIFTING

"Lack of results typically don't stem from a lack of resources, but rather a lack of courageous effort."

Intermediate athletes occasionally self-sabotage their confidence, preparation, and efforts through blame-shifting. "I don't have enough time!" "My coach didn't tell me!" "It's too far away!" "There is nowhere to train!" Shifting accountability is dishonest, immature, and cowardly. These qualities aren't found in champions.

Habitually shifting blame results in a loss of self-respect, increased poor performances, and decreased confidence in abilities. Avoidance of taking responsibility becomes contagious and contaminates all aspects of one's life. In an effort to console the athlete, it is very common for parents and coaches to comply with their athlete's blame-shifting behaviors to lessen the burden.

Parents who blame shift after their child's losses unknowingly teach them how to fail consistently and comfortably.

Parents and coaches need to stand firm and constructively call out blame shifting and resist the temptation to augment the athlete's excuses. It is critical to reinforce the learning experiences gained through proper training and competition and not condemn mistakes or failures. Athletes maximize potential with continued learning. Learning often comes from failures. Accountability is an essential life skill in successful individuals, and though some athletes may need to fail by first choosing the wrong path, it is incumbent that the coach and parents rein in poor behaviors sooner than later.

Blame shifting results in being ill-prepared for battle.

LEARNING FROM LOSSES

"Great competitors lose hundreds of matches throughout their junior, college, and professional careers."

It's usually through match play experience that we improve the software components. Under pressure, we become conscious of our limitations. Athletes, if they choose to do so, learn through losses, which makes losing a necessary part of the growth process. Progress requires appropriate mistake making and the acceptance of losses.

A past student of mine is Sam Querrey. He officially turned Pro in 2006. Sam plays in approximately 30 events annually and has won 10 ATP tour titles in the past 12 years. Sam's win-loss ATP record to date on tour is 354 wins-288 losses. Although Sam goes home losing most weeks, he's earned about 12 million dollars in prize money alone. That's a winner to me!

It's important to note that in order to win a 64-draw event (singles and doubles), athletes have to compete in approximately 20 sets in one week. When was the last time your athlete played 20 sets in one week? How about 10 sets? How about 5 sets?

If your athlete is not regularly playing practice sets, it's unlikely they are practicing in the manner they are expected to perform and properly to prepare for pressure.

EVERYONE NEEDS A MENTOR

"There's no need to go-it-alone."

Whether you're a coach, parent, or athlete, having an experienced and trusted adviser is key. Role models and mentors can save thousands of wasted hours, frustration, dollars, and tears.

Raising a champion is never a solitary pursuit. If you're a parent, seek out parents who've been through the junior tennis wars. Coaches, contact successful veteran coaches. Athletes, take an experienced champ out to lunch and discuss how their developmental plan differs from yours.

Vic Braden was my close friend (or "Pal" as he would say…), trusted advisor, and 25-year mentor. While working under him, he taught me, inspired me, and encouraged me to write my own books.

Finding mentors can make all the difference. The old saying, "It takes a village" is spot-on accurate when preparing for pressure.

CULTIVATE GRATITUDE AS A DAILY ATTITUDE

"Comfort stems from a grateful mind."

Some athletes thrive in those pressure-packed moments. How? By simply loving being in those big moments. They want to play on court #1, center stage, in the finals with a packed house. These exceptional athletes prepare for pressure by applying gratitude daily.

Without getting too fluffy, preparing athletes for pressure demands nurturing gratitude life skills because grateful people are mentally and emotionally healthier individuals.

So what are the benefits of gratitude? The attitude of gratitude will benefit your athlete by providing:

- An Optimistic Viewpoint of Every Situation
- More Connections-Friendships/Partners/Networking Opportunities
- The Ability to Focus on Fewer Physical Aches & Pains
- The Need to Chase Less Toxic Emotions
- The Ability to Handle Gamesmanship
- Greater Self-Esteem/Confidence
- Reduced Ranking Comparisons
- Appreciating Versus Resenting Other's Accomplishments
- Reduced Fear, Stress, and Nervousness
- Resiliency in Overcoming Hardships

Gratitude studies in sports psychology found significant links between gratitude and well-being. Mental and emotional strength is what every athlete seeks. Before bed, ask athletes to build their 'gratitude muscle' by completing a gratitude journal.

According to a study published in *Applied Psychology: Health and Well-Being*, even after devastating losses, being grateful fosters the resiliency to bounce back quicker and stronger. Spend five minutes jotting down a few grateful sentiments before bed quiets the restless, unsatisfied mind. Nurturing gratitude is a daily gift one gives to oneself.

A grateful mindset better prepares the athlete to handle pressure.

ATTITUDE IN BATTLE

"It's impossible to be grateful and angry simultaneously."

Athletes who routinely choose to play grateful versus angry have a distinct advantage under pressure. A proactive attitude helps players perform in the flow state they desperately seek but unintentionally destroy.

Even with the best of attitudes, athletes need emotional preparation. Pushing your athlete past discomfort on the practice court is often a heated affair. It's much more difficult than the typical snow job tennis lesson witnessed at the country club. *(Snow job: An avoidance of the real issues as the coach simply flatters the student until their lesson time runs out).*

Preparing for pressure consists of building the competitors emotional walls of defense. This competitive development includes both delivering big weapons as well as taking repeated hits. As the famous boxer, Mike Tyson says, "Everyone has a plan until they get punched in the face."

"It ain't how hard you hit. It's how hard you can get hit and keep moving forward." Rocky Balboa

THE COACHES PATHWAY

"I'm not going there," says Coach Kathy. "That's way above my pay grade. Little Kelly is nuts! Her Mom will get upset and blame me if I don't continue to just feed balls. Things will get uncomfortable, and they'll fire me! I'm just gonna ignore the white elephant in the room. I'll just hit & giggle and keep the paychecks coming by keeping the sessions lite & fluffy!"

The Coaches Pathway was written to emphasize the importance of teaching software skills, which can be a daunting affair for many teaching professionals. Coaches like Kathy, who lack the skills to teach software, or are unwilling to develop the mental and emotional components in their athletes, place their needs above their developmental obligations. Teaching software is not easy and is often rejected by both parents and athletes, who mistakenly judge the quality of the training session by the number of balls hit!

At the intermediate level, solid strokes get the athlete into the event. And together with fitness, the athlete progress through the early rounds. However, the athletes that consistently thrive versus wilt in the final rounds have well-developed mental and emotional components.

Successful coaches of the future will have developed the skills to teach emotional aptitude along with exquisite strokes.

MANAGING TRAINING TIME

"Value isn't directly correlated to volume."

Quantity versus quality of training is an underrated affair. Each minute isn't equal to the next. Effective time management is essential in a deliberate, customized developmental plan. In regards to maximizing a student's potential at the quickest rate, training should be intensely focused on the individual's unique needs.

If athletes aren't getting the results they're capable of, it may be the perfect time to design a new developmental plan.

I've witnessed expensive training sessions ranging from total time-wasting games to fun/socialization, to the development of skills and the repetition of those skills. While they all offer value, mastery of an individual sport requires a tailor-made, personalized plan.

Properly preparing for pressure requires evaluating the athlete's competence and confidence.

TOURNAMENT TIME PREPARATION

"People who fear the unknown focus on what could go wrong. People who welcome the unknown focus on what could go right."

For most people, unfamiliarity breeds stress. Preparing for the pressure of competition includes de-stressing conversations that flip the uncertainties into certainties. Anxiety is detectable through awareness in casual conversations. Once anxiety is recognized, strategies can be put into place to defuse the situation.

De-stressing conversational topics to discuss at tournament sites may include:

- The Surroundings, Court Speeds, and Weather Conditions
- The Athlete's Health Concerns/Injuries
- Performance Goals and Expectations
- Self-Destruction Solutions
- Refocus Strategies
- Clear Performance Goals
- Opponent Profiling (When possible)
- Routines and Rituals
- Nutrition and Hydration

Talk through solutions to anxieties to ease the athlete's nerves.

PRACTICE MAKES PERFECT ...
OR DOES IT?

"Practice Makes Permanent."

The old school saying "Practice Makes Perfect" is not exactly true. Experience tells us that practice makes whatever you're attempting permanent. Grooving flawed strokes only make the flaws permanent. One of the differences that separate the good from the great is in how they practice. There is a world of difference between effective training and ineffective training. Deliberate, customized training focuses on improving strengths and re-routing weaknesses versus mindless grooving.

So, how do we customize training? I recommend starting by videotaping actual matches and quantifying the data. Researching why points, games, sets, and matches are won or lost.

Great coaches use match data to improve:

- Opponent Profiling
- Between Point & Changeover Rituals
- Focus/Emotional Control
- Athlete's Top Patterns
- Cause of their Errors & Winners

Maximizing potential at the quickest rate is not typically found on the assembly-line practice court. It's not just about how to hit a stroke, it includes when, where, and why.

Those who progress quickly don't solely focus on repeating what they already know on the practice court.

DEVELOP COMFORTABLE ROUTINES & RITUALS

"Preparing for pressure requires making the unknown ...a little more known."

Navy SEAL's report that they spend approximately 85% of their time preparing for battle and about 15% of their time in combat situations. Their routines and rituals put them in the best possible position to handle extreme pressure. Routines and rituals are found in the four major components of our sport - the development and repetition of strokes, athleticism, mental, and emotional realms.

Simulating stressful scenarios in practice is a daily routine Navy SEAL's and competitive tennis players share.

Developing software skills is serious business. Under stress, athletes have to manipulate their software in order for their hardware to function correctly. For example, athletes must know how, when, and why they need to be able to calm down their nervous system to allow their fluid strokes to flow.

Poor emotional control can override the best mechanics and strategic intentions.

THE ART & SCIENCE OF PREPARATION

"Confidence under pressure stems from the individual's proper preparation."

Learning how to prepare for competition can be a challenge because it's so individualized. Before tournament play it is important to provide athletes with the physical, mental, and emotional skills needed to manage their performance. The depth of their game-day warm-up routine depends greatly on the quality of preparation leading up into the event. Catastrophe strikes when the athlete's pre-event preparation is less than optimal, and their warm-up is minimal.

Sadly, I hear the following parental statement all too often, "My Jenny takes a half-hour private every 2-weeks, and I drive her all the way to the high school to hit in the hour-long clinic every Tuesday and Thursday. If she gets in the upcoming National, I think she should win the title!"

Of course, high-performance athletes train differently than Jenny. I'll say it again, preparing for pressure includes: incorporating the perfect storm of strokes, court speed, endurance, proficient strategic patterns, tactics to oppose the various styles of opponents, and performance anxiety busters.

Readiness requires the continuous refining of each skill essential to competing under pressure.

PRESSURE REVEALS CHARACTER

"Be the alpha predator...not the prey."

All predators can smell fear and uncertainty. They sense the timid and weak, and they prey on them. The predator could be a lion on the plains of Africa, the hoodlums on the subway in NYC or the experienced tennis competitor.

Alpha competitors can be physically, mentally, and/or emotionally imposing. Mark Twain once said, "It's not the size of the dog in the fight ...it's the size of the fight in the dog."

The key mental/emotional characteristics of tennis predators include:

- The ability to hit the shot the moment demands.
- The unwavering belief that they are the best.
- A strong demeanor, assertiveness, and dominance.
- Calmness and supreme confidence in the moment.
- Resiliency, perseverance, and grit at crunch time.

Learning to read fear and taking proper advantage of the situation is one of the hidden mental/emotional differences that separates the consistent winners from the pack. Walking into a clubhouse before the match, victors and victims may look similar but possess polar opposite mentalities.

**Teach your athletes not to be afraid of the storm
but to be the storm.**

MAKE CROSS TRAINING AND ATHLETICISM MANDATORY

"Getting fit solves many problems."

Cross-training improves muscle strength, cardio, cognitive processing, and mental clarity. Enjoying off-court training sessions alleviate stress and enhance overall well-being. Getting fit is known to improve mental health by raising the athlete's mood-boosting endorphins. As fitness increases, attitudes improve, and perceptions change. Confidence builds as it quickly assumes control and takes action.

There is a cumulative effect that comes with getting into killer shape and mastering a new skill. Physical, mental, and emotional improvement is seen within just a few weeks. It's important to note that tennis is a flexible skills sport and not a consistent skills sport. Meaning, tennis competitors have to be trained to make millisecond decisions requiring brain speed as well as foot speed.

Anticipation without hesitation is a skill which is needed at the higher levels of competition.

Tennis groundstrokes have been measured at 100 mph and serves have been clocked well into the 150 mph range. With these facts, players must have anticipatory skills to compete at the higher levels. The mental action of anticipating, expecting, or predicting is much more critical than ever. The art of anticipation should be a part of every coach's curriculum.

Court speed is a combination of foot speed and brain speed.

SPOTTING ANOMALIES

"You can't spot competitive tendencies by simply feeding balls to your students."

Profiling athletes begin with spotting anomalies. I like to start the analysis by observing them playing a set. My initial focus is on two main issues: what is currently present that shouldn't be there and what is not present that really should be there. Anomalies are components that deviate from what is standard, normal, or expected at the higher levels of the game.

My internal coaching inner dialog includes:

- "Is he patient or impatient?"
- "What's her shot and frustration tolerance levels?"
- "What are his stroke weapons and weaknesses?"
- "How's her foot speed, strength, and endurance?"
- "How's his cognitive processing speed and focus ability?"
- "Does she apply between point rituals and problem-solve?"

One of my favorite ways of gathering information to prepare athletes for pressure is identifying trends within the cause of errors. In competition, errors stem from four leading causes: poor form, reckless shot selection, inefficient movement/spacing, and of course, negative emotions/focus. Errors may also be the result of a combination of the four causes.

Why is spotting the cause invaluable? If 22 of the athlete's 28 backhand errors were caused by reckless shot selection, would feeding balls right into the athlete's strike zone and continuing to perfect their form be the appropriate training pathway? Not likely.

Preparing for pressure requires identifying both the athletes winning and losing trends.

DOES TENNIS CHARTING AND ANALYTICS MATTER?

"Solid analytics spot winning trends and reoccurring nightmares."

Statistics in tennis is currently in vogue, but it isn't necessarily new. While teaching at The Vic Braden Tennis College/Coto Research Center back in the 1980s, I was involved in multiple statistical chart studies. Computennis was a tennis-based analytics group that also did wonderful work in this field 40 years ago. These research projects looked deeply into "quantifying data" in various levels of play. We uncovered basic stats that still hold true today. One is the average length of points in singles (3.8 hits) and doubles (2.9 hits). Another vintage stat identifies the most missed shot in the game: Return of serve (which is also still the least practiced shot in the game). A third old school stat that still holds true 40 years later is that approximately 70% of errors are located in the net.

Although analytics don't tell the whole picture, they have greatly affected my students' lesson plans since the 1980s. I've designed specific match charts to assist in preparing serious athletes for competition. These simple to use analytics provide more in-depth data than the typical phone apps and guarantee to improve your athlete's win-loss record. Samples Include:

FIRST STRIKE WINNING PERCENTAGE:

The First Strike is the very first shot your athlete hits- serve or return of serve. Identifying the winning percentage of the location of your player's serve and return of serve (First Strike) is shot selection awareness which benefits strategical play.

BETWEEN POINT RITUALS CHART:

This chart identifies the player's ability to stay focused and execute their critical between point rituals. Players who do not keep their brain focused on the task at hand have to defeat two opponents-the opposition and their own wandering mind.

CAUSE OF ERROR CHART:

Tennis is a game of errors. The first most critical step in error reduction is to spot the actual cause of the error. This chart will require you to identify the cause of the error. This information leads to the customization of future lessons. Note: the four leading causes of errors are poor technique, poor movement, reckless shot selection, and negative emotions/focus.

COURT POSITIONING MATCH CHART:

This chart will differentiate whether playing "reactive" tennis from behind the baseline earns the best winning percentages or whether playing "proactive" tennis from inside the court increases winning percentages. Note: The court position your athlete prefers to play may not be the position that wins them the most points.

MEGA POINT CHART:

Mega points are the game-winning points. This chart is especially important in competitive tennis because it highlights the game-winning points. Tipping a close match in your favor requires spotting a big point before it's actually played, paying attention to match details and running the smartest patterns.

SERVING PERCENTAGE CHART:

This chart discriminates between the different essential factors required to hold serve, serve consistency, serve location, and first and second serve win-loss percentages. Ask your player to let go of the "speed" of the serve and begin to focus their attention on the above components. Note: On the WTA tour, second serve win-loss percentages are the most critical factor in deciding the outcome of the match.

Note: While applying analytical data, keep in mind exceptions shadow every rule in life, so customization is key.

(The Match Chart Collection by Frank Giampaolo is found at www.maximizingtennispotential.com)

Solid analytics through match charting can assist in spotting winning trends as well as reoccurring nightmares.

SOFTWARE IS DEVELOPED
THROUGH PEER CHARTING

"Researchers have long known that the best way to understand a new concept is to explain it to someone else. To quote Seneca, a famous Roman philosopher, 'What we teach, we learn.' Scientists have labeled this learning strategy, The Protégé Effect."

The Match Chart Collection is a tool that brings this ancient wisdom to the tennis competitor. Match charting provides innovative methods for athletes in group tennis sessions to engage in a deeper understanding of the mental and emotional complexities of competitive tennis.

The Following Lists Advantages of Match-Charting Skill Sets:

1. Students who are charting and teaching (explaining their results) accept and retain more than the athletes who are hitting. Why? Because they're focused on the details of the match while the hitters are typically focused on the outcome.
2. Match charting provides non-threatening data acceptance.
3. Researchers have found, student-athletes enlisted to teach others to work harder to understand the intricacies of the game, recall it more accurately, and apply it more effectively.
4. Athletes who chart their peers develop a higher tennis IQ and EQ.
5. While charting, athletes increase their self-awareness and solution-based problem-solving skills.

6. Students gain significant insights into designing customized game plans.
7. Charting skills enhance the athlete's opponent awareness skills.
8. Students gain confidence by charting, which reinforces their capacity for handling pressure.
9. Interpreting match data requires tactical dialog between students, which is an essential interactive learning skill.
10. Peer charting elicits teamwork and cooperative learning, which makes charting a powerful instructional tool for group sessions. It exposes the gaps in your athletes match awareness. Apply peer learning with the revolutionary Match Chart Collection by Frank Giampaolo to analyze performance and skyrocket your competitive practices.

Athletes don't learn the mental skills by grooving strokes. They learn them through being exposed to analytics.

MENTAL REHEARSALS TO ENHANCE PERFORMANCE

"Desensitize anxieties by applying mental rehearsals."

One way athletes learn to respond with solutions is through visualization. The use of imagery recreates the positive experiences athletes need when seeking confidence. Overcoming the onslaught of stressors is much easier if the athlete is desensitized to the situation.

Successfully dealing with uncomfortable scenarios in a relaxed environment helps to prepare the warrior for the battle ahead. In the studies of performance psychology, mental rehearsals are proven to facilitate real-time match performance. *Neuro Priming for Peak Performance* is a dedicated workbook I wrote to assist athletes as they apply customized mental rehearsal scripts. These scripts are then recorded into the athlete's cell phones and listened to nightly and before competition.

Prepare for pressure by visualizing clean stroke mechanics, millisecond decision making, shot sequencing patterns, and between point rituals, to name a few.

Pre-match visualization desensitizes anxieties and improves performance.

THE IMPORTANCE OF PROPER BREATHING TECHNIQUES

"Proper breathing boosts performance."

Josh, a witty student of mine said, "Come on Frank! It sounds a bit silly that you are reminding me to breathe. What next? Reminding me to blink? Look, coach, no offense, but I've been breathing my whole life effortlessly!"

Without oxygen freely flowing to the muscles, lungs, and brains of our athlete's, catastrophe is likely to strike. The following scenarios result when deep breathing routines and rituals are not implemented:

- Fluid strokes stiffen
- Athlete's body tightens up and often cramps
- Fatigue sets in prematurely
- Core stability lessens
- Anxiety levels increase
- Concentration levels diminish
- Problem-solving skills decrease

In match play, there are two phases of correct breathing techniques.

During Points Phase: Educate the athlete that inhaling begins while tracking the incoming ball and during the coiling phase of the stroke. This energizes the uncoiling links into impact. Exhaling at impact relaxes and loosens their "swoosh" swing, as it grounds the athlete and stabilizes their strike zone.

During the Between Points & Changeovers Phase: Educate the athlete to switch their focus on the benefits of applying calming, deep breathing techniques. By slowly breathing through their nose, the athlete will lower their heart rate as they take in greater amounts of oxygen into the bloodstream.

This, of course, provides physical, mental, and emotional benefits such as increased energy, sharper memory recall, relaxed muscle exertions, reduced anxieties, calmer nerves, improved judgment, and decision-making ability.

Breathing properly during match play has emotional benefits as well. Athletes focused on their breathing techniques ward off contaminating anxiety that can creep into an empty mind. Correct breathing significantly improves performance under pressure.

Ask your athletes to play a few practice sets while focusing their attention on their breathing techniques. By simply paying attention to correct breathing, they are sure to boosts performance under pressure.

ORGANIZE CUSTOMIZED DEVELOPMENTAL PLANS

"A goal without a deliberate, customized plan ...
is just a dream."

Effective developmental plans are based on the athlete's competence levels, efficiencies, and deficiencies, as well as long-term career goals. Self-assessment is often inaccurate, so I recommend enlisting an experienced coach to provide feedback.

Athletes attending school routinely rotate from math to science to English - the school methodology. This structure produces well-rounded adults. Tennis training components are similar to school classes. Preparing for pressure requires the development of each component. Tennis instruction should consist of tennis-specific off-court/athleticism, primary & secondary stroke development, pattern repetition, sets, mental/emotional classroom sessions, match play video analysis, and tournament competition.

When a plan is in writing, you have the ability to track and measure the progress and hold the athlete and their entourage accountable for execution. Each plan should include goal dates to measure progress. Plan on revising the athlete's development plan every 3-6 months.

SAMPLE WEEKLY/DAILY PLANNERS

"Directing your future into the present makes your destiny come alive."

Sasha was a top-ranked 14-yr-old junior I worked with back in 2012 in Auckland, New Zealand. Sasha seemed to have everything going her way as she progressed through the ITF junior wars. She had athleticism, committed parents, a racket and clothing contract, and the backing of Tennis New Zealand.

Fast forward 7 years, and I run into Sasha as I was coaching at an ATP/WTA tour event in Israel. Sasha was emotionally struggling. As we went to lunch to catch up, she said "I'm quitting. I'm playing horribly, and I can't beat anybody." As we ordered our meals, I asked about her weekly developmental plan with her team of coaches. The conversation went like this:

Frank: *"Sasha, how many hours are you spending getting crazy fit? You know...in the gym and working on your cardio?'*

Sasha: *"Umm ..., I'm not training. It's too hard on the road, and at home, there aren't any good trainers."*

Frank: *"How's the repetition of your top patterns?"*

Sasha: *"Well, I can't practice my patterns because I don't want to pay a coach, and the other gals only want to groove back and forth."*

Frank: *"Sasha, you're 21 now, right? Remember when you were 14, and we talked about match play video analysis?"*

Sasha: *"Oh my, I haven't done that since then ...How funny!"*

Frank: *"Tell me about your weekly practice matches. Are you rehearsing your competitive skills?"*

Sasha: *"No …No one will play sets on tour, and there's nobody good enough to play with back home."*

Sasha's poor WTA results were caused by her series of weak excuses and bad decisions. I'm convinced that Sasha will once again thrive under pressure when she chooses to incorporate a continuous series of proper routines and rituals. (The name and country have been changed to protect the guilty.)

The estimated formula for a world-class individual is training approximately 20-hours a week for ten years: The 10,000 Hour Rule. The following weekly and daily training component tables provide a comparison guide to evaluate your athlete's training schedules versus that of a Top National Ranked 14-year-old athlete.

Please keep in mind customization is key. Quality trumps quantity.

WEEKLY DEVELOPMENTAL PLAN (Hours Per Week)	Yours	Theirs
1. Off-Court Gym (Core/Upper body)		3
2. Off-Court Cardio (Speed/Stamina)		3
3. Primary Stroke Production		2
4. Secondary Stroke Development		2
5. Pattern Development		2
6. Complete Practice Matches		4
7. Video Analysis		1
8. Audio Tape Visualization (Neuro Priming)		1.5
9. Serving Basket		2
10. Tournament Play		4
TOTAL Hours Per Week		23.5

SAMPLE DAILY PLANNER: Home School Example

Monday 2/11	Tuesday 2/12	Wednesday 2/13	Thursday 2/14	Friday 2/15	Saturday 2/16	Sunday 2/17
6:30 - 8:00 Off-Court Gym	6:30- 8:00 Off-Court Cardio	6:30 - 8:00 Off-Court Gym	6:30 - 8:00 Off-Court Cardio		8:00 - 9:00 Match Day Preparation	8:00 - 9:00 Match Day Preparation
9:00- 11:00 Primary & Secondary Strokes	9:00-11:00 Pattern Repetition	9:00- 11:00 Sets	9:00- 11:00 Sets	9:00-11:00 Pattern Repetition		
		11:00- 4:00 School Homework	12:00- 2:00 School Sets	12:00-3:00 School	10:00- 12:00 Tournament Competition	10:00- 12:00 Tournament Competition
1:00- 3:00 School	1:00- 3:00 School					
			3:00- 4:30 Primary & Secondary Strokes		2:00- 4:00 Tournament Competition	2:00- 4:00 Tournament Competition
3:30- 5:00 Sets	3:30- 5:00 Return Serve and Secondary Strokes			3:30- 5:00 Sets		
		5:00- 6:00 Serve & Return Drills	4:30- 5:30 Match Play Video Analysis		4:30- 5:00 Match Logs	4:30- 5:00 Match Logs
8:00- 8:30 Neuro Priming		8:00- 8:30 Neuro Priming		8:00- 8:30 Neuro Priming		

80

SAMPLE DAILY PLANNER: Regular School Example

Monday 2/11	Tuesday 2/12	Wednesday 2/13	Thursday 2/14	Friday 2/15	Saturday 2/16	Sunday 2/17
6:00- 7:30 Off-court gym	6:00 -7:30 Off-court cardio	6:00- 7:30 Off-court gym	6:00 - 7:30 Off-court cardio	6:30- 7:30 Pattern Repetition		
8:00- 3:00 School	8:00- 3:00 School	8:00- 3:00 School	8:00- 3:00 School	8:00- 3:00 School	8:00 - 9:00 Match Day Preparation	8:00 - 9:00 Match Day Preparation
					10:00- 12:00 Tournament Competition	10:00- 12:00 Tournament Competition
					2:00- 4:00 Tournament Competition	2:00- 4:00 Tournament Competition
3:30- 5:30 Primary & Secondary Strokes	3:30 -5:30 Sets	3:30- 5:30 Pattern Repetition	3:30- 5:30 Sets	3:30- 5:30 Serve & Return Plus 1 Drills		
		5:30- 6:30 Match Play Video Analysis			4:30- 5:00 Match Logs	4:30- 5:00 Match Logs
	8:00- 8:30 Neuro Priming		8:00- 8:30 Neuro Priming	8:00- 8:30 Neuro Priming		

INSTRUCT HOW TO AVOID COUNTERPRODUCTIVE BEHAVIORS

"Your Academy's culture is determined by how much counterproductive behavior the coaching staff is willing to tolerate."

Counterproductive thoughts and actions are behaviors that go against the interests of the athlete's progress. Successfully preparing for pressure demands re-routing poor choices. Athletes and parents are often loyal to their counterproductive behaviors simply because they've been doing them for so long.

Basic counterproductive behaviors include tardiness, lack of effort, lack of a developmental plan, indifference, pessimistic dialog, anger outbursts, blaming, and accusing.

I've found that athletes who possess these unproductive traits are often facing difficulties away from tennis. In these situations, the dysfunctional behaviors should be referred to medical professionals.

Red flags are seen when an athlete's words don't match their actions.

DISCUSS CONFLICT RESOLUTION AND FEAR OF CONFRONTATION

"Solving problems begins by confronting problems."

When athletes are expected to be the competitor, the score-keeper, the linesman, and the umpire conflicts will exist. "Being judged" can bring out the best and worst in all of us. Often opponents who believe that they don't have the physical tools to win employ gamesmanship to sabotage their opponent's level of play. There are many gamesmanship situations that athletes need to be aware of, and it is the job description of the coaching staff to address these scenarios. It is also important to teach them to look systematically beyond the incident.

Often, it is not the specific opponent's gamesmanship tactic but your player's response to the drama that causes the emotional break the opponent seeks. Preparing for pressure includes how an athlete responds to confrontational situations and whether or not they can remain focused on their performance goals and avoid unraveling.

Covert gamesmanship in tournament play is also applied when the crafty opponent spots the nonverbal clues found in our athletes' fear of confrontation. If your athletes have a fear of confrontation, address why standing up for themselves versus enabling the "bully" is in their best interest. Nurturing timid athletes to stand up for themselves improves their confidence as they learn to solve problems.

In the intermediate levels, emotionally weak competitors assume that confrontation is bad. If they disagree, the opponent won't like them and therefore not want to play with them in the future. This is a false assumption. In tennis, the opposite holds true. Opponents that can easily bully and beat your athlete don't return their calls. Athletes that stand up to gamesmanship and triumph, not only earn respect, they also benefit by getting to choose their future practice match opponents and doubles partners.

Confidence is earned through standing up to conflicts.

PURSUE EXCELLENCE VERSUS PERFECTION

"Excellence invigorates...Perfectionism demoralizes."

Perfectionists are motivated over-achievers pushing themselves to the highest standards. They believe their extra attention to detail and long hours of hard work will produce the perfect athlete who can replicate perfection in every performance. These standards are impossible to meet, so these individuals often get caught in a toxic spiral of failure. Loyal to that nurtured perfectionistic view, they suffer needlessly.

To prepare for pressure, it is in these athletes' best interest to allow a little wiggle room and shift their impossible goal of consistent perfection to consistent excellence. Excellent performance is attained when an athlete plays close to their current peak performance level throughout tournament play.

Striving for tennis perfection has many drawbacks, such as slow cognitive processing speed which leads to hesitation and tight muscle contractions. This emotional state produces slow racket head speed and poor risk management due to the fear of failure.

Top ATP Professionals such as Federer and Nadal routinely win about 53% of the points they play annually. They make mistakes in each match. They don't need to be perfect, and neither does your athlete.

IT PAYS TO EDUCATE THE PARENTS

"Throughout this book, the term 'Educated Tennis Parent' refers to those parents educated about the tennis developmental process."

Three Reasons for Educating Tennis Parents:

1) Educated tennis parents will help build and maintain a winning program, which directly benefits the athlete, the parents, and the club's program.

Uneducated tennis parents shift alliances blindly from academy to academy, coach to coach as well as USTA/ITF/UTR sanctioned events. These uninformed parents damage the cohesiveness that a successful developmental program offers. Uneducated parents unknowingly waste incredible amounts of time and finances, chasing points around the globe.

2) Educated tennis parents will assist in developing team synergy and family harmony. Resulting in a more optimistic and supportive understanding of the process, which directly benefits the athlete, the parents, and the club's program.

Uneducated tennis parents can sabotage and confuse the athlete's developmental process, pre-match preparation, ranking, and the effort of a quality coach.

3) Educated tennis parents will be accountable **"TEAM MEMBERS"** and assist in facilitating a deliberate, customized developmental plan which directly benefits the athlete, the parents, and the club's program.

Uneducated tennis parents don't understand their detailed job descriptions or those of the entourage and may unknowingly sabotage performance, obstruct the athlete's developmental plan and create havoc.

Athletic accountability begins with parental accountability.

THE PARENTAL VISION

The Parental Vision was written to assist parents in shaping their athletes future. What parents think, say, and do matters. In my experience, a parent obsessed with character trait development and positive brainwashing trumps the parent obsessed with pointing-out their athlete's failures.

Issues arise when the parental influence is misaligned, which confuses the athlete and derails the process. It is important that the athlete, parents, and coaches are all on the same page with the singular goal of maximizing the athlete's potential.

Parents who shape their athletes future make the journey a family priority. This section includes samples of goal setting and advanced scheduling.

"A goal without a plan is just a dream."

The parent is the team leader who's responsible for shaping the athletes future. Parents only interested in being passively involved should only expect average results from their children.

Parents, children model the behavior they witness daily. It's not only what you say ... it's what you do that matters most.

PARENTS, DO YOU HAVE A PLAN?

"Your Weekly Initiative Separates Your Athlete From Their Peers?"

All throughout the history of tennis, we have seen ordinary men and women come from humble backgrounds with nothing but a dream. Most of these athletes weren't especially gifted or financially wealthy. Yet they were able to become top ATP and WTA professionals. What separates us from them is their family commitment to push beyond mediocrity. It doesn't take much effort to be average. Follow the crowd, and you'll reach that level.

Most athletes dream of playing professional or NCAA ball but only a few are destined for greatness. It's estimated that only 5% of High school varsity tennis players move on to play high-level college tennis. It's not their lack of athleticism, it's their lack of a deliberate, customized developmental plan.

The tennis success you seek requires a high tennis IQ, well developed emotional aptitude, and the acceptance of serious weekly growth.

FIND THEIR WHY

"The willingness to prepare is more important than wanting to win. Preparing to be great begins with WHY?"

Mr. Jones wants the new S500 Mercedes Benz with jet black exterior and the baseball-mitt brown leather interior. To afford such a luxury, he realizes he has to work overtime for the next few years. Mr. Jones found his "Why" (his new dream car), so he's happy to put in the extra at work.

Junior athletes need to choose between being a champion or a "normal" kid. They also need to buy into their "WHY"-intrinsic motivation. I recommend planting the seed of athletic royalty at the college of their choosing. Review the common perks of the typical college athletes such as free books/laptop, priority registration, room & board, full time dedicated tutor, and of course, tuition!

The multiple benefits and rewards of participating in college tennis may be the reasons why young, intelligent athletes put in the daily work.

CONFIDENCE STEMS FROM CULTURE

"Parents, your thoughts and emotions are highly contagious."

The parents are the athlete's most consistent sphere of influence. Parents can help prepare athletes for pressure by priming confidence through solution-based optimistic dialog. They should also model positive life skills daily.

Parents would be wise to nurture their athlete's software (mental and emotional skills) as much as they expect a hired coach to develop their child's hardware (strokes and athleticism).

Let's look at a typical week. We all get 24 hours a day, seven days a week. That's 168 accountable hours. If a high-performance athlete is training their hardware with their coaches for approximately 20 hours a week, how many hours are left for parents to assist in the software development? The remaining 148 hours a week offer wonderful opportunities for mental and emotional growth.

Being clutch at crunch time is a learned skill. Understanding how to thrive versus wilt under pressure is developed by master coaches and master tennis parents. Another great question parents should ask themselves:

Is someone routinely mentoring the mental & emotional protocols needed to handle pressure in competition? If not, consistent disappointment is sure to shadow most upcoming tournament competitions.

Parents, if you're not developing incredible character traits, a moral compass, and essential life skills, who is? Preparing for pressure requires the development of the athlete's software skills.

Parents are the athlete's most consistent sphere of influence.

THE CULTURE OF BELIEF

"If you keep working this hard, you'll be playing at the US Open!"

This was my actual weekly battle cry to my stepdaughter. By the age of 15, Sarah was competing at the US Open. The typical parental pre-match pep talk sounds like this: "Today's so important! Don't blow it again! You have to win!"

Belief stems from habitually using life skill terms such as effort, fight, resiliency, courage, persistence, and focus. Parents should routinely apply these lure words to subliminally planting the seeds needed to be clutch under pressure.

Molding belief is similar to molding memories. Do you remember hearing a childhood story throughout your youth that actually never really happened the way it's told? These embellished accounts spun by family members eventually become real memories. Similarly, parents can apply a form of positive brainwashing to motivate athletes to believe in themselves in the heat of the battle. Children are impressionable. It's within the tennis parent's job description to convince their athletes that they can and will succeed.

Nurturing life skills and positive character traits should be every parent's daily battle cry.

100

MOLDING THEIR INNER VOICE

"Parents beware: Your thoughts and words become your child's beliefs, and their beliefs become their actions."

Leading into competition, great parental dialog from a non-tennis playing parent includes de-stressing and confidence building banter. High IQ tennis parents can review software solutions. These performance reminders are both mental and emotional. Mental triggers to discuss may include the athletes "A" game plans, contingency plans, their script of essential patterns, and opponent profiling.

Emotional triggers to discuss before matches may include solutions to performance anxieties, how to handle "creative line callers," how to stop self-destructive performances, and how to close out a lead. Optimistic self-coaching in match play stems from molding the athlete's inner voice. It is the counterforce needed to reverse the habitual pessimistic internal dialog that sabotages peak performance.

Taming the critic that lives inside the athlete's parents is essential in preparing the athlete for pressure. This parental metamorphose doesn't happen overnight.

TEN QUESTIONS PARENTS SHOULD ASK THEIR ATHLETES

"Ask...don't tell."

Let's begin with identifying the number one question parent's should NOT ask, "Did you win?" This question pulls the athlete into an outcome-oriented mindset, instead of being growth-minded. The art of communication with athletes includes promoting accountability and problem-solving. Commanding your child what to think is a sure-fire way to encourage disconnection. It's our job to show them where to look, but not to tell them what they see. Teach your athlete to analyze their performance and to research solutions which promotes growth and retention.

Questions Parents Should Ask:

1. How was your preparation?
2. How do you feel about your performance?
3. What worked well?
4. What can you improve?
5. What did you learn?
6. How else would you have handled that?
7. What would you do differently next time?
8. Are you satisfied with your level of play?
9. How was your composure under pressure?
10. Did you thank your coaches?

Competitive tennis is incredibly emotional. Parents, it's within your job description to share your calmness versus partaking in their chaos. Your child needs to hear, "I want to hear your opinion. I believe in you. I'll always be here to help you."

IDENTIFYING YOUR PERSONAL STRESS RESPONSE

"When results matter, pressure will affect performance."

Parents, ask yourself, "Is performing under pressure beneficial or harmful to your child?" Your answer determines how likely you are to be affected by competitive pressure. Because of that, your athlete will likely inherit that point of view. If the parent perceives pressure as a negative force, they will repeatedly associate it with anxieties such as negative judgment, fear of failure, and self-doubt. Parents applying a pessimistic viewpoint drains the athlete's energies before competition even begins. Uneducated parents pull the athlete's focus away from performance goals and into the praise or criticisms coming their way.

This common negative parental mindset leads to the dismantling of the trust every good coach develops. All too often a stressed-out parent unknowingly sabotages the confidence they've just paid a coach to instill. Once tournament titles are perceived as paramount by the parent, the process of performing when it matters most is shattered.

It's meaningful to understand how stress multiplies. The design of a tournament draw ensures that pressure increases through each round of the event. As the level of stress increases, so to must the athlete's emotional aptitude. Pressure naturally increases towards the end of each game, set, and match. If the pressure begins to be perceived as overwhelming the performance level will decline. Monitoring and releasing pressure stems from the proper use of between point rituals and changeover routines.

Athletes who choose to skip these "recharging stations" routinely breakdown when they need emotional clarity the most.

What if pressure was seen as beneficial? Billy Jean King famously said, "Pressure is a privilege." An optimistic point of view is that the athlete is where their peers want to be. Athletes who are nurtured that pressure has positive forces become unflappable at crunch time. These balanced parents who are routinely nurturing tenacity and confidence have athletes who apply situational awareness versus outcome obsessions.

The impact of parents greatly influences the athlete's physical, mental, and emotional development. In the correct optimistic frame of mind, pressure prompts growth, and consistent growth is what you seek. So, is pressure seen as harmful or beneficial to the development of your child?

Promote competition as an information gathering mission necessary to test developing skills.

IS THE PARENT A SOURCE OF EXTERNAL PRESSURE?

"It's no secret that a large portion of pressure comes unknowingly from tennis parents."

The tennis parent is the second most important entity in the athlete's entourage (The athlete being the most important.)

The parents are the CEO, the manager of the entourage of coaches, and the facilitator of the players customized developmental plan. With responsibility comes pressure. This is especially true when the parent is bankrolling the journey. All too often, tennis parents become overbearing yet don't see themselves as the leading source of frustration.

Communicating with an adolescent competitive athlete isn't easy. A relaxed demeanor versus a stressed appearance matters deeply. In fact, current studies show that approximately 7% of communication is verbal, while 93% is made up of tone of voice, facial expressions, and body language.

While it's natural for parents to be on high alert for any possible signs of danger, it's essential to understand that the athlete needs a calming influence.

Parental pressure can be both real and imagined. In the end, it's the perception of the athlete that matters.

UNDERSTANDING INTERNAL PRESSURE

"Thriving under pressure requires exposure not avoidance."

Teaching a junior competitor to handle internal pressure is a complicated affair. It greatly depends on their genetic predisposition. Some personality profiles are wired to over think, worry, and stress, while others are natural-born competitors. If your athlete wilts under pressure, this is for you!

A solution that will help athletes to become comfortable in match play is replacing the mindless grooving of strokes in the academy with actually competing in real practice matches. Organize your athlete's training sessions to focus on competitive, simulated stressful situations on a daily basis.

After a solid foundation is built, redundant technical training is counter-productive. Preparing for pressure demands exposing the athlete to more live ball flexible skills training. This allows them to make the software mistakes and learn from them on the practice court long before tournament play occurs.

A second solution in preparing for pressure is to avoid always enrolling your athlete in events above their actual match play level. I recommend also registering your athlete into lower level, winnable tournaments. This will allow them to gain the much-needed experience of playing longer at their peak performance level six matches in a row. Athletes need to routinely experience what it's like to compete in the semis and finals of events.

Athletes need to become accustomed to the physical, mental, and emotional symptoms and cures found in real match play. Only with experience will they learn how to perform under pressure.

Parents, it's your job to fluctuate your athlete's exposure to the different levels of competition at the correct time. Their tournament scheduling should be customized to their current needs.

KEEP YOUR ATHLETE ON-SCRIPT BEFORE COMPETITION

"Your athlete's script is their repeatable dominant patterns."

Let's go a step deeper into how parents can assist their athletes in preparing for pressure. When your athletes are uncertain, they play confused and fearful. Fear is the enemy of peak performance. When your athletes and their coaches design scripts (with clear physical, mental, emotional protocols), these intentions breed confidence. Focusing on their script of pre-set patterns and solutions serves two purposes for the athlete.

The first benefit is that a proper headspace distracts the athletes from the onslaught of contaminating outcome thoughts. Worrying about the possible upcoming catastrophe gets most athletes into a horrible mindset. While they can't really stop themselves from thinking, you can purposely distract them from outcome dreams and nightmares. It's important to note that often, the parents are the instigators of the contamination.

The second benefit is strategic- pre-setting rehearsed patterns and plays prior to competition. This is accomplished by asking your athlete to review their current performance goals, strategies, and contingency plans. Mental rehearsals through visualization is a terrific way to assist the athletes to adhere to their script mentally and emotionally before competition.

Great performances begin with an optimistic organized mindset.

PARENTS, AVOID DISCUSSING OUTCOME GOALS

"On match day, to reach outcome goals, avoid talking about them."

Many athletes add stress before competition by discussing outcome goals. Such conversations include, "I should beat Zoe 1 & 1, she's only ranked an 8 UTR", "I'm going to prove to my coaches and friends that I'm better than Mathew," "I should easily reach the finals in this tournament!" The focus on these unnecessary outcome goals only adds unwanted stress to a stressful environment.

Similarly, parents are also to blame for destroying the calm mindset athletes seek. Parents often unknowingly add their own outcome-oriented stress as they routinely talk about "you should easily be hitting 2 aces a game with the service lessons I paid for this week!", "This opponent is a pusher. You should win easy.", "Once you win this tournament the USTA will have to invite us to the National Campus to train!"

These topics hurt the athlete's chances of reaching their desired outcome. Instead, leave the speculations at home and choose to focus on the strategic performance goals customized for the upcoming match.

Desired outcomes are found when the entourage manages the performance.

PARENTAL SABOTAGE

Meet the Kolouski's – A familiar Mother/Father duo who unintentionally sabotage any real chance of their daughter playing at her peak performance level.

Martha Kolouski Saturday Morning Pre-Match Routine:

- Wakes up tightly wound.
- Doesn't like Kelly's choice of outfit.
- Upset about her chewing at breakfast.
- Peeved about the poor directions.
- Annoyed about catching every red light.

Martha's at the end of her rope & Kelly's match is still an hour away. Guess who is sabotaging any real chance of Kelly performing at her peak performance level?

After Saturday's poor performance, Mark decides to take Kelly to the event on Sunday.

Mark Kolouski's Sunday Morning Pre-Match Pep Talk:

- Ok, Kelly…she's ranked 98 spots ahead of us.
- Our ranking will skyrocket into the top 20 - if you don't blow it!
- Remember, she cheats and will push- so focus!
- This is the most important match of the year for us - by far!
- We spent $2000.00 to get you here….so don't expect us to keep on forking over hard earned money if you lose!

Once again, guess who is sabotaging any real change of Kelly performing at her peak performance level?

TEACH THE VALUE OF KEEPING PROMISES WITH YOURSELF

"False promises are a form of self-sabotage."

Confidence is built when athletes know they can rely on themselves. The top contenders that I've had the privilege of working with routinely matched their intentions and their actions on a daily basis. Procrastination and excuses are left to the weaker players. The fragile athletes avoid keeping promises.

Improvement typically stems from changing behavior. And changing behavior requires a commitment to training. Athletes choosing not to keep their commitments with themselves are destined to suffer when the pressure begins.

Athletes who have problems with matching their words with their actions would be wise to commit to a simple 30-day challenge. The task is to complete a 5-minute nightly journal. Listing five of their tennis related daily accomplishments that will significantly assist them in staying on track.

Often junior players say, I want to be a top player. But their actions say I want to be a normal kid. It is important to remind athletes that they cannot be a Champion and a normal kid. They have to pick one because the pathway to becoming a Champion is far different than the path for normal kids.

Keeping promises makes the athlete ... Breaking promises breaks the athlete.

TRUE HAPPINESS STEMS FROM PROGRESS

"Seek daily progress versus daily perfection."

As crazy as it sounds, true happiness doesn't always come from winning. It comes from performing at one's peak potential under pressure.

Did you ever win a match against a player whose ability was levels below yours? It wasn't truly satisfying, was it? Did you ever compete against a player whose ability was several levels above yours and you played amazingly, only to lose in a tightly contested battle? Remember walking away proud of your performance?

Choosing to feel passionate about performance as opposed to the outcome opens the doors to progress. Only with constant progress is consistent victory insight.

Let's do a comparative analysis: 32 girls play a weekend soccer match and 16 players go home losers, and 16 go home winners. The same weekend 32 girls play a junior tennis tournament and one player wins, and 31 go home losers.

Tennis families that are only happy if they win the whole event are not likely enjoying the journey.

ENCOURAGE SMILING, LAUGHING, AND HAVING FUN

"Adding ranking pressure is sure to add the exact performance anxieties, great coaches work hard to avoid."

Parents, if you make the junior ranking race too important, you'll quickly see your athlete's performance diminish. When rankings are seen as more important than fun, athletes suffer. Preparing for pressure involves creating a culture of gratitude and enjoyment. Athletes who perform at their peak level in competition are first and foremost having fun. Enjoyment is the secret ingredient that assists the athlete when they need it the most.

De-stressing the athlete comes from promoting growth and weekly progress over the outcomes of events. After events, routinely discuss 3 successful aspects of your athlete's performance and 3 improvement goals. Win or lose, celebrate the performance goals hit, and then get to work on the development of the athlete. According to brain function analysis in sports, performing calm when it matters the most is a creative, right-brain dominant affair. Athletes pulled into their editing left-brain typically suffer due to overthinking under pressure.

Parents, coaches, or athletes who make a match too important witness the athlete's ability disappear. When the outcome overshadows the enjoyment, catastrophe strikes.

INSIGHTS FOUR

PERFORMANCE ANXIETIES

Most athletes experience performance anxiety. It's only natural when being judged. Performance Anxieties Insights were written as a guide to problem-solving real-life fears through exposure versus avoidance. Exposing an athlete in practice to match-day stressors helps to desensitize the athlete to their anxieties.

Each player's genetic predisposition and their upbringing play critical roles in the amount of stress they choose to suffer.

Often at tournaments, I witness role models (parents and coaches) who are far too focused on the outcome. When this occurs, the athlete is sure to follow with timid play, which is a sign of an outcome-oriented athlete on the verge of self-destruction.

On a deeper level, we as parents and coaches want our athletes to experience consistent, daily satisfaction. This type of long term happiness doesn't come from winning tennis trophies. Instead, it stems from constant, daily growth. Confidence skyrockets only when the athlete's effort and parental praise is placed on improvement versus winning. By focusing on the effort versus the outcome, performance anxieties are diminished. Let's look at a few common performance anxieties.

"I DON'T WANT TO PLAY, WHAT IF I LOSE?"

"Devalue the event to deflate the anxiety."

A common outcome-oriented mindset is that each tournament is a life or death crisis. This negative frame of mind is counterproductive and incredibly stressful. It would be wise to educate the athlete and their entourage that tournament play is only an information-gathering mission. Each match should be analyzed to determine why they won points or lost points as a result of their competitive decisions. The objective is simple, quantify the data and learn from it.

Competition should be seen as a fun challenge, not intensely difficult or dangerous.

Destress the situation by decompressing the athlete.

"I HIT FOR 10 MINUTES ... I'M READY!"

"Prepare both hardware & software components for battle!"

Preparing for pressure demands more than merely warming up one's fundamental strokes. The week leading up to the event is a terrific time for the athlete to organize their clothes, equipment, and nutrition and hydration requirements. For example, early preparation allows leeway if the athlete unknowingly is out of his favorite strings or their lucky shorts are in the wash.

Come game day, I recommend athletes prepare their mental and emotional components by reviewing their pre-recorded audio tapes the morning of the match. Complete a dynamic stretch and warm-up their primary and secondary strokes with multitasking movement. (Hitting on the move instead of just standing still.) Prior to checking in, hydrate and go for a short run to reduce anxiety and warm-up the body.

Preparing for pressure requires the confidence that comes from complete preparation.

"SECTIONALS ARE NEXT WEEK. MY COACH WANTS ME TO CHANGE MY FOREHAND?"

"Before competition gain confidence in your existing skills."

Proper preparation begins weeks leading into the event. During this prep phase, avoid significant mechanical changes or adding brand new concepts. Why? It takes approximately 4-6 weeks for a new motor program to override an old one. If a stroke is dismantled at the wrong time (right before competition) the athlete's old motor program is shattered, and their new one isn't developed yet.

Remember when getting grooved used to be called muscle memory? Be careful using that term "Muscle Memory" because nowadays even the 10 & under crowd know that memory isn't stored in their muscles.

The bottom line is that the days leading into an event are not the correct time to introduce a new skill. Starting a new routine may cause the athlete to become confused, sore, or injured, and the required recovery time is not available. Many coaches and parents are unknowingly guilty of poor periodization.

Five customized phases of development are recovery, analysis, general training, competitive training, and competition.

"EVERYONE SAYS, 'JUST PLAY YOUR GAME,' BUT I DON'T KNOW WHAT MY GAME IS?"

"Top contenders have defined their global style & most proficient patterns of play."

Upon arrival at a coaching gig in Spain, I noticed the coaches on all the red clay courts running the same drill. Player A hits a high & heavy ball deep to player B's backhand. Player B retreats, contacting the ball above his/her shoulders and produces a short reply. Player A moves into no-man's land and screeches "AHH ...HEEE" and drives a winner into the open court. I asked the famous director, "What's the drill they're all working on?" He laughed and said, we call it, "How to beat the Americans."

Athletes should start each match with their global style of play. Whether they're in Miami or Moscow, in the first round or finals, on hard or clay courts, starting matches by doing what they do best is an intelligent formula. Their global system is their most proficient style of play (not necessarily their favorite style). Styles include hard-hitting baseliners, counterpunchers, retrievers, and net rushers.

The athlete's global system also includes their repeatable strategic plan – which is their most proficient patterns of play. These patterns need to be designed and developed. They include: serving and return patterns, rally patterns (like the above Spanish group), short ball options, and net rushing plays.

In competition, each athlete has to know what they do best and must routinely apply their global plan and hitting the same old, boring winners over and over.

Every player should know and have had rehearsed their strongest, repeatable patterns of play. Then, choose to play those patterns in matches.

"IT'S NOT MY STROKES THAT FAIL ME; IT'S MY MENTAL TOUGHNESS. I JUST FREAK OUT!"

"Mental toughness is often confused with emotional toughness."

My definition of mental toughness in the tennis world is the understanding of strategies, tactics, and patterns. It also includes opponent profiling and problem-solving skills. My definition of emotional toughness is the ability to overcome the onslaught of performance anxieties and outcome-oriented emotional thoughts.

Solutions to match issues begin with understanding the actual cause of the problem. Is the athlete's above statement: "I just freak-out!" A mental issue or an emotional issue? I would say it is an emotional issue. Because the correct solution is customized to the cause of the problem. I recommend digging deeper into why this particular athlete "freaks out." Does it involve the above mental categories, emotional categories, or a combination of the two?

It's important to note that a seemingly unrelated component may be the root of the athletes break down. For example, if an athlete is physically unfit for serious competition, that lack of fitness can cause stroke mechanics to break down, reckless choices in shot selection, and manifest negative emotional outbursts.

Preparing for pressure involves knowing the difference between the mental and emotional components.

133

"HOW DO I SPOT WHEN I'M LOSING FOCUS?"

"Be on high alert for signs of mental detachment."

In matches, it's not uncommon for athletic individuals to realize that the opponent isn't the only cause of their losses. It's their roller coaster performance. Their detachment fuels bouts of sloppy play which complicates even the most routine matches. So, how can a player spot when their performance level is about to take a dive?

The following are 10 common signs of an athlete detaching from their script.

1. **Unfocused Eyes:** "Are my eyes starting to wander outside my court?"

2. **Reckless Shot Selection:** "Am I now attempting shots the moment doesn't really demand?"

3. **A Drop in Intensity:** "Has my energy level or focus intensity dropped?"

4. **Frustration-Body Language:** "Am I calm or agitated?"

5. **Rushed /Panicking Play:** "Is my breathing shallow and is my heart racing too fast?"

6. **Choking/Pushing:** "Am I worried about the outcome?"

7. **Lack of Rituals**: "Am I skipping my between point rituals?"

8. **Hesitating**: "I know how to play my game, but am I chickening out?"

9. **Attempting to Play above Your Level**: 'Do I really need to hit this big?"

10. **Wandering Mind**: "Am I thinking about irrelevant, contaminating thoughts?

If detachment is spotted, disconnect and reboot before returning to play. Verbal and physical triggers pull the athlete back on script. Verbal triggers include "Get back on script." "One point at a time." Physical triggers involve moving your feet and doing some loose shadow swings.

Reconnecting to the correct headspace starts with picking up these available clues.

"HOW DO I REBOOT AFTER A BAD PATCH?"

"What defines a competitor is how well they get up after they've fallen."

Bouncing back quickly from heartache is what separates the competitive contenders from the pretenders. Having the courage to accept the situation and adapt is the resiliency you seek. It's important to welcome the fact that competitive tennis matches are routinely stressful.

How to reboot when things get uncomfortable falls into the software department. Reconnecting to peak performance is done through slow/deep breathing, match tendency awareness, optimistic inner dialog, visualizing solutions, shadow swings/footwork, refocusing the eyes, and taking more time with relaxation rituals.

When the going gets tough, don't be afraid to reinvent

"JOHNNY SCREAMS AND THROWS HIS RACKET, WHY CAN'T I THROW MINE?"

"Attitude and emotions are highly contagious."

Remember the old saying, Monkey See Monkey Do? It's human nature for people to model themselves after their sphere of influences subconsciously. Behavior modeling is a form of social learning. It states that most behaviors are picked up through imitating who and what they see.

Preparing athletes for pressure include carefully navigating athletes away from bad influences. Bad influences can sabotage the strong character traits you seek.

It is the athlete's responsibility to detach themselves from anyone or anything that pulls them away from the progress they seek.

Be aware of the behavior of those influencing the athlete.

"I'VE LOST CONFIDENCE. HOW DO I GET IT BACK?"

"Your positive performances are imprinted in your memory, so choose to re-live them."

A re-occurring defining characteristic of champions is their strong software skills. There are many times in a professional athlete's career when they've lost their confidence and had to reboot their motivation.

One solution lies in choosing to focus on past successes more than past failures. Failure is no doubt part of the learning process but revisiting past successes via- match video analysis is one method used to rekindle self-esteem. If you don't already videotape tournament play and analyze your performance with an experienced coach, now's a great time to start.

Past successes leave a footprint in the brain. Remind yourself of previous pressure-packed situations when you performed spectacularly. Go into detail. Where did it happen? What event? What round? How did I overcome the challenges? Why was I determined to fight? What was my inner dialog and mindset? This process stops the discouragement and replaces it with the realization that you've done it before and you'll do it again.

Preparing for pressure comes from realizing that you have come through under pressure before.

"IT'S LOSING TO THE WEAKER PLAYERS THAT KILLS ME... I SELF-DESTRUCT!"

"Self-destruction unknowingly begins in the preparation phase."

The worst part about the feelings of self-destruction in competition is that the athlete is fully aware it's happening but can't do anything to stop it. Their muscles begin to tighten, they shank every other ball, and their brain is fixated on contaminating outcome thoughts. We've all been there. You're choking, and you know it, the opponent knows it, even the spectators know it, but you weren't taught any self-destruction solutions, so the match feels like a slow death.

Rehearsing self-destruction solutions on the practice court provide the athlete with a practical "go to system."

The following are a few proactive solutions to employ during match play to aid in regaining focus:

- Focus on Hitting 3 Balls Deep Down the Middle
- Apply the Old School Bounce-Hit Method of Vision Control
- Return to your Script of Top Patterns of Play
- Reboot your Between Point Rituals

I recommend the player choose two of the previous solutions and play a few practice sets, and focusing exclusively on the selected solutions to stop imploding behavior.

Preparing for pressure requires pre-set solutions to common problems.

"I USED TO BEAT THESE TOADS...NOW I'M LOSING TO THEM."

"Regrouping begins by reassessing current efficiencies and deficiencies."

When athletes are no longer getting the results, they believe they're capable of, I recommend conducting an honest assessment of their current training and match preparation. With few exceptions, I find that the athlete has changed their developmental routines and not for the better. In these situations, a fresh start makes a world of difference.

I'm a bit more detailed than the average coach. When I'm hired to revive a stalled career, I begin with a 300 Point Assessment of the athlete's life skills, weekly developmental routines, primary & secondary strokes, mental skills, emotional skills, and incorporate match video analysis. Together, the athlete and I assess their confidence level, under pressure in each category. By doing so, we relaunch their progression with a new deliberate, customized developmental plan.

Revitalizing a career begins by organizing the athlete's developmental plan.

"IN REAL MATCHES, I'M SO STRESSED. ALL I THINK ABOUT IS DON'T LOSE ... THEN I LOSE!"

"Internal dialogue refers to the unspoken conversations we all have ..."

Athletes are often unaware of the inner conversation they have through the course of a tennis match. Internal dialog is the conversation our ego is having with ourselves. In match play, inner dialog takes place in-between points and during changeovers. This is when athletes are encouraged to program themselves towards a more constructive mindset. With between point ritual practice, athletes will learn to focus on what they want versus what they don't want.

It's true that society propagates a negative bias day in and day out. Athletes would benefit from committing to replacing the typical negative statement, "The problem is ..." with "The solution is ..."

Positive self-coaching revolves around a reoccurring theme of this book: Gratitude. It shifts our mentality from pessimistic to optimistic. I encourage my athletes to apply the mantra: There's nowhere I'd rather be than right here, right now!

Energy flows wherever their internal dialog goes.

"I FOCUS THE WHOLE MATCH ON PERFECT FORM. THAT'S CORRECT ...RIGHT?"

"Athletes nurtured to focus on mechanics in match play seldom perform in the flow state."

I recommend that athletes save most of the detailed analysis of strokes for the improvement phase, which takes place on the practice court. Biomechanical analysis surely has its place; it's just not in the midst of competition. Focusing too much on "bend your knees," "close the racket face 30-degrees and brush up," and "tuck the left hand in on the serve to block the third link of the kinetic chain" pulls athletes out of the flow state and into their editing, analytical brain.

The week leading into an important event, I recommend trading-in the need for stroke perfection and replace it with practicing picking up relevant cues like proficient pattern play, score management, and opponent profiling. This prepares the athlete for pressure by allowing their judgmental ego to slip away. Performing in the zone requires relaxed contentment, which can't be found if you're focused on fixing every micro-flaw.

Preparing for pressure requires the athlete to focus on the art of competing.

"YEAH, I KNOW I SHOULD PRACTICE MORE, BUT I'M TOO BUSY."

"It's not the most gifted athletes who typically succeed; it's the most organized and disciplined."

Preparing athletes for pressure include pointing them in the right direction. One of the assessment tools I use is the 168 Hour Rule. We all get 24 hours a day, seven days a week, equaling 168 hours. I ask junior athletes to begin with 168 hours a week and then deduct their hours for sleep, school, homework, and other serious interests. Most often, the very same athletes who claim that they're too busy realize that they have 60-70 free, unaccountable hours weekly. This exercise is very eye-opening for both the parents and the athletes.

After we identify the athlete's free time, we re-design their weekly developmental plan. Together we assess the quality of the hours they're dedicating to their long-term goals.

An example of a typical conversation after reviewing time assessment may go like this, "Joey, since you just revealed that you have 60 unaccountable hours weekly; would it be possible for you to increase your deliberate customized tennis training to 20 hours a week? That'll still leave you with 40 hours a week to hang out with friends, socialize, and play video games!"

Growth stems from managing one's time efficiency.

CONCLUSION

It's obvious to me that if you've read through to the end of this book, you're committed to something very special. What ultimately matters is not how much money we make or how many trophies our athletes hold up, but what we have sacrificed for the development of future generations.

In my opinion, the greatest tennis teachers don't just teach stroke mechanics, but they teach courage, confidence, compassion, and the long list of emotional skills that will significantly benefit their athletes throughout their lives. Teaching positive character traits has a cumulative effect. It doesn't just enrich the life of the singular athlete but everyone they touch.

The United States is starting to see the enormous impact educating life skills has on millennials. There is a new online movement across the country called: Adulting Classes. High Schools are even starting to catch the trend. In these courses, real-life education and preparation is the curriculum. I wholeheartedly agree that these tools are missing in today's young adults.

My intention is for ***Preparing for Pressure*** to assist athletes on and off the courts. I hope that this book enriches your teachings and helps create lasting memories. Not just your memories, but the great memories that will live on in your children and students.

ABOUT THE AUTHOR

Frank Giampaolo is an award-winning international coach, popular international speaker, and sports researcher. He is an instructional writer for ITF (International Tennis Federation) Coaching & Sports Science Review, UK Tennis Magazine, PTR Tennis Pro Magazine, the USPTA, Tennis Magazine and Tennis View Magazine. Frank is both a USPTA and PTR Award Winning educator, a Tennis Congress Faculty Member, and has been a featured speaker at the Australian Grand Slam Coaches Convention, the PTR GB Wimbledon Conference, and Wingate Sports Institute (Israel.)

Frank is the bestselling author of Championship Tennis (Human Kinetics Publishing), The Tennis Parent's Bible (Volumes I & II), Neuro Priming for Peak Performance, The Soft Science of Tennis, Raising Athletic Royalty, and Emotional Aptitude In Sports. His television appearances include The NBC Today Show, OCN-World Team Tennis, Fox Sports, Tennis Canada, and Tennis Australia.

Frank founded The Tennis Parents Workshops in 1998, conducting workshops across the United States, Mexico, Israel, New Zealand, Australia, England, Canada and Spain.

Frank's commitment to coaching excellence helped develop approximately 100 National Champions, hundreds of NCAA athletes, numerous NCAA All-Americans and several professional athletes. His innovative approach has made him a worldwide leader in athletic-parental education. Frank is currently the Vice Chair of the USTA/SCTA Coaches Commission.

Contact Frank Giampaolo:
(949)933-8163
FGSA@earthlink.net
www.MaximizingTennisPotential.Com

Facebook:
http://facebook.com/FrankGiampaoloBooks.The Tennis Parent Bible

Google:
http://plus.google.com/u/0/+FrankGiampaolo/posts

Twitter: http://twitter.com/@Frank_Giampaolo

Made in the USA
Coppell, TX
21 January 2021

48556370R00087